# *The* TEMPERANCE TALE

## Julie Modla

Published by Amazon UK

www.juliemodla.com
Cheshire, United Kingdom

ISBN: 9798714481840

# SOULS CHOOSE ROLES

Souls, choose roles and right from the start.
Like all good actors, get lost in the part.
Forgetting true nature, from whence they have sprung.
Forgetting the reasons, for which they have come.
Forgetting the author, forgetting the plan.
There's few to remind them, this aint what 'you' Am!
There's few to remind them, there is much more
than this.
To trigger their internal curiousness, but should it
be triggered, there's no turning back.
For the stage starts to wobble, the scenery cracks.
And what seems so solid, is not anymore.
The actor remembers there was a stage door.
Through which they gained entry, to play out
their role,
In a long running saga...the path to the soul.

*Anonymous*

# SAMUEL HARRIS

Money. How is it that those, who have plenty, feel guilty, and those who have very little, feel ashamed.

Such was the case of Samuel Harris who married for it; only to find out its true value, far too late.

Samuel Harris had done rather well for himself. His upbringing had been a grim one. Not the most affluent, to say the least, not by anyone's standards.

The area where he lived with his mother, father and three younger sisters was anything but inviting. Grey, cobbled streets with small little houses crammed together with no privacy from the neighbours. Washing, hung out to dry across the alleyways. Some, no more than rags of different shapes and sizes. A man's shirt swayed in the wind, it looked no cleaner than if it had been rinsed through a dirty puddle.

A woman shouted and chased two young boys onto the street as they played a game of running through her pristine white sheets, leaving their grubby handprints behind. She swore she would blind them if she got hold of them.

Some of the windows were cracked and broken had been stuffed with bits of cloth into the cracks. While a girl with bare dirty feet played swinging round the lamppost on some rope.

The welfare reports had stated that the houses weren't fit for habitation as the downstairs were overrun with little black beetles that would scatter when a lamp was lit. Either that, or else sleep upstairs with tiny red bed bugs. Crimson dots stained the walls around the beds, where little ones had squashed the little beasts, in the hope that they wouldn't get eaten alive by them.

When all was said and done, living here had given Samuel the drive and hunger to succeed, and to steer his wheels onto the right path. It had given him direction as to what he didn't want his life to be. His imagination and vision were about to shape his future.

It was to the envy and astonishment of his family and friends, and those within his close circle. That this poor boy, whose family were evicted, who were turned out onto the street. Their landlord, turfed them out when his father lost his job for being drunk and disorderly.

Thrown out on the streets as a young man, not even being able to pay the rent, on that slum on the outskirts of Manchester. Samuel vowed and swore to himself, that he would never experience such hardship ever again.

Rehoused within another place of poverty. Samuel knocked on every door he could, to find himself a job. He managed to secure a position, working for a local mill owner. Work shy he wasn't, and after a hard day's graft, he would arrive home truly shattered. Nearly every penny he earned he paid into the family household, as he vowed that from this day forth, he would keep a roof over his and his family's head.

A small portion of his earnings he kept aside, which enabled him to pay for violin lessons. A small indulgence, but to the distress of his family. They covered their ears, to the shrieks and scratches, as Samuel's bow scraped away, as he desperately tried to master the strings. The hardships he had experienced would shape his future.

He worked his way up alright. becoming Edwin's right-hand man. He had gained the confidence of his employer, and due to his good nature and hard work. Samuel was given a promotion to mill manager and this is where his luck, very soon changed.

Some said the sun always shone on Samuel Harris. However, he would have argued that it had all been down to luck, and his own hard work.

He had charmed and won the heart of Eva, Edwin's daughter and after a fairly short courtship, had asked for the permission and blessing from Edwin to marry his daughter.

So that was what happened next. Samuel, married into the mill trade that following spring. He had proved himself to be a good honest worker, and an excellent manager of the mill.

Delighted to be on the mill owning ladder,

he followed in his father in laws footsteps, and became a very wealthy man, anyone who had the fortune to be employed by Samuel Harris, were safe in the knowledge that as long as they abided by his rules, they would be more than well looked after.

Shortly after they wed, they were gifted with a child, Grace. Doted on by both her mother and father.

A good man and a salvationist. The town he inherited had been built around the mill.

Samuel was a regular church goer, he had strict rules that he enforced within the town surrounding the mill, there were to be no licensed venues, at all, as he believed this is where all the trouble started with employees. Beer and brawls were a detriment to an honest day's work.

He had heard rumours that places of drink; were where the trade unions of the times, grouped together, to cause trouble, and that would never do.

Plus, he didn't agree with intoxication, as that was how his father had lost his job, and even worse, lost the roof over his family's head. So, the long and short of it was; all those who worked for Samuel Harris, had their rents paid, good wages, health care, all perks of the job, and all the houses were owned by the mill.

The accommodation was of very good solid stone. Built to last for years. Each one had its own privy in the back yard, no communal toilets for his tenants.

He had taken the liberty to name streets after royalty and famous people, with the presumption that they would jot the dates in their calendars when the streets would open, then he would invite them to stay at his grand abode.

Newspapers and journalists would be

tipped off, as to who was visiting, and the tabloids, would fall over themselves, to get a scoop.

Samuel, was influential, and as long as people worked hard he would continue to employ, and give his employees a decent standard of living. His own little empire, right there within the north of England.

Edwin, the original mill owner had a soft spot for his new son in law, a boy he had never had. When Edwin passed, it was a sad day for all, Samuel promised his father-in-law on his death bed that he would look after their little empire.

Eva was a beautiful quiet soul. A real contrast to Samuels larger than life and jovial personality. This, he concluded was the recipe as to how they got on so well, real opposites.

He still practiced his violin, his party piece. His guests were thrilled at his performance.

Deep down his wish was to have been famous and played solo on a stage in front on hundreds.

There were lavish parties. Never any shortage of good food and drink for his distinguished friends.

Eva on the other hand forced herself to join in with her husband's festivities but was always relieved when they, the guests had left and she could withdraw to her own space and the tranquillity of her books and her garden.

Blessed with that one child. Grace by name and grace by nature. Born in 1941. A war baby, her heart shaped face and adorable green eyes were unique.

Samuel wanted many more children but as Eva was of a delicate disposition, they counted their blessings, and were happy that they had been gifted with one.

Sadly, Eva passed away with consumption when Grace was only five.

From then on Samuel devoted his time and energy into bringing up his daughter, with the help of paid staff. The child wanted for nothing and very soon, grew into a gracious young lady.

Grace was to have the best of everything. Schooling, that Samuel could never have dreamt of as a boy. Grace, wanted for nothing. He loved this child with all his heart. Unconditionally.

She was to receive the finest ballet lessons. French was taught by Madame Gabriella and piano tutoring by no other than Sergei Petrovitch. Not a penny was spared.

Grace was trained and presented into London's society as a young woman.

Forced into attending a stuffy ball with his parents the Lord and Lady Ashbridge of Cheshire. Freddie was captivated by Grace's demure and dignified aura.

Freddie had been born with a silver spoon

in his mouth. Or so some would say.

Quite early on as a young boy, he had begun to rebel against his privileges. Yearning for a more ordinary life.

As their relationship blossomed, Samuel had his doubts. Even though her suitor was from an aristocratic background. With good-breeding and money, what more could a father want? No one was ever going to be good enough for Samuel Harris's daughter. The boy, he worried was a bit wayward and too much of a rebel.

Freddie, courted Grace. He was always on the guest lists at all of the top night clubs of the day. He was popular with the bands, and was seen in all the right places.

Grace learned lessons that only Freddie could teach her. How to let her hair down and be herself. To lose the stuffiness that her parents had inflicted on her.

It was on that eventful day, that Freddie

crunched his new bottle green sports car, up along Samuel's driveway. With the roof top down, Freddie arrived care free. His daughter had been eagerly waiting for her boyfriend to arrive. He was always so fashionably late, to her frustration.

Today, she wore a pale blue shift dress made from some deliciously flowing fabric with matching earrings. Her long dark hair had been secured in a chignon, her Hermes head scarf, tied beautifully just to stop it flying all over the place. Grace ran to meet her boyfriend as he jumped with agility out of the car, and opened the passenger side for her to step in.

Samuel smiled lovingly at his daughter then just as quickly looked on with a disapproving face, as Freddie, jumped back in the car and driving to impress, stepped on the gas and sped off her father's drive, and on into the warm summer's afternoon.

Freddie and Grace drove on as the sun set behind them, heading for the one of the newest and best restaurants in Town. The Wisteria, where Freddie showed off, ordering the finest food and champagne.

They were an extremely attractive couple who could certainly turn some heads, wherever they went.

No expense was spared.

Then on to one of the elite nightclubs of the time. Freddie was always on the guest lists, where they would drink and dance for hours. Partying to the vibes of the swinging sixties. Grace was in awe of his sense of adventure and his recklessness. She hung on to every word he said and laughed at all of his jokes.

Grace had well and truly fallen for this man's charm. Freddie dabbled in a lifestyle that was all exciting and unknown to her.

The warm night breeze intensified as they

drove through the country lanes and back into Cheshire. There was a lay-by at the side of the road and Freddie pulled over the car as he needed to relieve himself.

Grace stepped out to stretch her legs as they had been driving for an hour or so and rested herself on the bonnet of his car.

Freddie returned from the undergrowth and his eyes eased her slender silhouette. Her face was turned upwards, as she took in the night stars.

A hazy mixture of cologne and him, stirred her senses. He had poise and self-assurance. His sense of ease, as his fingers curled around hers. He aroused in her a feeling of safety, and danger. He brought out feelings that were new and exciting to her.

Hypnotic, the strength and feel of his frame leaning in. He pulled her towards him, by the small of her back, as he pressed her hard against him.

'I won't, if you don't want me too' he teased, as his thumb gently brushed her lower lip and he stared into her eyes.

Lips searched lips and he kissed her with a softness at first. The scent of the nights air mixed with champagne added to her intoxication.

Clinging to him, he deepened the intensity as he pulled her in closer. Her fingers subconsciously slipped under his shirt and there, they were both lost in time. A moment only the two could share.

~~~

Samuel was woken up suddenly. To his annoyance, by a loud knocking on his front door. He glanced at the time, the numbers lit up in the dark as luminous green paint, reflected the numerals on his wind-up clock.

It was 2.45 and as he rubbed his tired eyes, he begrudgingly made his way down his grand staircase, to the sight of blue lights, flashing within the grounds of his property.

Incomprehensible and agonising. No one wants to see a policeman stood at the door at that time in the morning.

The next time Samuel would see Grace, was to formally identify her. Her chest still, he hoped there would be a flicker of life there, but instead he was met with the cold silence of deaths embrace. Now to be incarcerated within a small wooden box. Her life abruptly ended. Her skin and her bones mangled within a wreckage of metal.

The lad had desperately and frantically tried to free Grace from the carnage, but to no avail. Her internal organs were crushed.

The headlines in the Daily Wire read: *Grace Harris was killed in a tragic car accident.*

*After returning home from an evening out in the city. Her boyfriend Frederick Ashbridge, son of Lord and Lady Ashbridge of Cheshire, lost control of his sports car during a freak summer thunderstorm. The driver had a lucky escape and walked away from the wreckage with minor injuries.*

*Her family paid tribute with a moving statement released this morning.*

*Grace was described by her father as a bright and wonderful daughter.*

*'Words cannot do justice as to how I feel right now. The days and weeks ahead will lay heavy on my heart, no joy and no hope. Each day will be as bleak as the next, as I hadn't been there to do my basic duty, to protect my beautiful daughter.'*

Freddie had been drinking heavily the night before and was in no fit state to be behind the wheel. His family were well acquainted with excellent lawyers and the judge and after the trial. Freddie walked away with a ban and a hefty fine, which his father took care of for him.

Samuel was now forever in chains. A beautiful house, everything monetarily he could ever wish for. Enslaved, cuffed by his inability to let go of his daughter.

His last memory of her cold and alone, a shell; cleverly made up so the bruises to her face were disguised.

The memory of the sound, the casket made, that final thump, as it was lowered into the cold dank earth. Jolting him to the core as the finality hit him like a brick.

Samuel Harris pleaded and begged to the Divine for answers. He felt compelled by his grief to turn away from his faith, as he believed that he was being punished for his lavish lifestyle.

He spent days and weeks looking through his daughter's photographs with a gripping fear in his gut, that he would forget her face and the enchanting sound of her beautiful voice.

A strange sort of guilt, that he had a hand to play. He had helped in some way to create this stage show.

The dreams were vivid, so real; some acting out happy times with her, playing in the garden, laughing and running. Only then to waken and endure the nightmare once more.

Yes, he would visit the place where she had been laid to rest. One day as he sat on the bench near her, a voice came into his right ear. 'I am here, father.' Startled, but in a strange way, reassured, he turned quickly as he was sure she was standing right behind him.

As time went by, he would try to let go of his pain, only for it to resurface with a vengeance. Becoming pensive, a contrast to his usual self.

A great agony would consume him. His jovial persona had been suffocated and muted, only to reveal himself, as a melancholy old man.

Unable to move forward from his grief and pain he numbed his thoughts, with fine wines and ports and resided within his own space to play his heart out upon his violin.

Samuel never did get over the death of Grace his beautiful girl. He felt he didn't have much to live for after that.

All the money in the world couldn't bring him happiness now, he was lonely; oh yes, there were many a female that desired his company, but Samuel knew only too well, what for.

When that damn scoundrel Freddie had come on to the scene, Samuel had warned Grace, many times. The rumours that circulated, but she wouldn't have a bad word said about play boy Freddie.

His pleading had been in vain, as he warned her to be careful, the more that fellow, charmed Samuel's daughter and just like putty in his hands she fell into his arms.

On reflection he now realised, that it was out of his power to want for her.

That young man taught Grace to love and be liberated. He had taken her to places that she would have never dreamt of going if it hadn't been for Freddie.

In her short life she had experienced more than most. The privileges that her upbringing had brought, and her short encounter with that aristocratic young racing car driver. Enticed and excited the senses that Grace had never known existed.

Samuel still couldn't help finding himself in a deep dark place of despair, as he still didn't think he had done enough, to prevent

Grace's death.

He had struggled with his hate for Freddie for a long time. The fact that he had walked away from the carnage with barely a scratch. He did believe that Freddie, loved his daughter. He was also aware, that his daughter's lover, would have the crash, the horrific memories of her death, on his conscience for the rest of his life.

Samuel had, had conversation, after conversation with himself, as he felt his own actions had caused her death alongside Freddie's.

Had he not searched for a better life, and had he not married for money, it would have likely been a different outcome. His daughter would have never become involved with that man.

After finding a small amount of peace in that knowledge, Samuel did however eventually return to his faith.

It was on a cold October morning, Samuel was found slumped on the chaise, by his hired help, a handful of Imipramine close to his half empty decanter of cognac.

The toxicology report confirmed that Samuel had 1000g of this toxic antidepressant in his blood stream at the time of death.

A drug he had been prescribed to help lift his mood, he had used to numb and join his loving family.

*Who is rich and who is poor; I have begged as a poor boy on the streets, and I have begged to god; a rich man in a chapel.*

*I now lay down here and take my ease, the sands of time drain from an hour glass as the curtain goes down with nothing left to see.*

*A broken melody on earth, I carry on to the sweet music of the Divine.*

Samuel then dreamt of his wife who he was so very fond of. He embraced her once more.

Grace ran to his open arms; she was a child once again. Spinning her around within his beautiful garden, his little girl back home with him safe and sound. Back home with his family.

His soul searching had concluded this human experience had been planned on a soul level very long before; happy to return to his family, with many lessons learnt.

An extremely clever man, who had worked his way up from the slums of Ardwick. Always been in control, had now taken charge of his very own destiny. Once again a happy man.

# CYRIL REYNOLDS

A vocation that only the brave would have chosen. His ideology was that he was serving society. Helping to rid the public of the dregs. The only trouble was, not everyone walking to the drop was necessarily guilty.

He took great pride in his work, he had the belief that it was his responsibility to ensure the condemned, met a swift death with speed and efficiency. With bodily suffering minimised.

He had grown up in a working-class area. The son of a coal miner, no airs and no graces, 'get yourself up at the crack of dawn and earn a crust for the table.' His father would say.

He had a fascination with detective novels and would read all he could on crime, and catching the villains. He had always liked to read these novels, ever since he was old enough to borrow books from the public library.

If his secret would be known, he had always fancied himself as a bit of a Hercule Poirot, if he was honest.

Cyril's dad liked to shoot an odd rabbit or two and he would often go off with him, he had taught him how to aim his gun and fire, a good shot, and how to kill the prey quickly and swiftly. So not to cause any distress for the poor beast. He wouldn't kill the game for sport, or anything like that, it was more to put tea on the table.

It was a friend down the pub, that mentioned, the government were recruiting and there was good money to be made, so long as you didn't have a faint heart.

The position was for an executioner.

A hangman to be specific.

Cyril had recently married and was trying to make a few pounds aside from the job his dad had fixed for him in the colliery.

He didn't think too much about whether he had the stomach or the mental stamina for the role. He applied for the position and was very surprised when a few weeks later, he received a letter from His Majesty's Prison informing Cyril that he had landed himself an interview.

Brigadier Alan Bates was his interviewer. Cyril, quite a confident chap under normal circumstances, found himself to have suddenly developed a stammer. Over thinking his responses to the Brigadiers questions.

When the Brigadier finally asked him about his hobbies, Cyril was on a role; his knowledge about the prison service and the detective novels he had read and the stories he had absorbed over the years, increased his confidence and he was away. He had finally found a subject, close to his heart and he struck up rapport with his senior.

He left the prison, feeling fairly confident, went home and waited in anticipation for his reply.

A few weeks later, the letter he had been waiting for arrived, he had been accepted as an apprentice to become a public executioner.

His training would start the following month, and he was to travel by train, to Strangeways prison.

On entering this place, the smell of school dinners mixed with sweat and disinfectant. The unnerving clinking and clanging as he was locked into this institution with the inmates. A claustrophobic feeling as he realised, he could only walk out of this place when his shift was over and even then he had to rely on a key holder to let him out.

It was quite an unnerving experience as he was aware that there were those in here for petty theft and robbery, in contrast to those who had committed atrocities and would kill you, as soon as look at you.

He followed the senior officer and his colleague to the condemned cell. He was surprised how small it was. He was advised that they would be staying above the cell, and to be quiet as the prisoner would spend his last night without disturbance.

Many of the condemned were surprised to find the execution chamber doors were only ten paces away from their cell. The room was an identical size to the condemned cell, A lever resembling that at a railway station to the right of him, on looking up there was a solid beam, and below his feet, a trap door.

He was ordered to stand back and the doors smashed loudly open, there were steps leading down into the basement. As he ventured cautiously down he was aware of two exits. One lead to a cold, pristine mortuary room and one led to the prison grounds.

Cyril and his colleagues would open a flap in the door to see the prisoner through a window as he or she took their daily exercise. They would ask for the age, the height and the weight of the prisoner. This would allow them to gauge the drop for the execution.

He would work with his superior, they would check the execution chamber and prepare. There would be a dummy run with a sack the size and weight of the prisoner. As every shape and size had a different drop.

You see, the problem was, a person aged 25 with a weight of 9 stone, strong, with a muscular shape would have a different drop to a person aged 68, 9 stone with feeble muscle tone.

A linen hood was used so that the prisoner wouldn't see the executioner reach for the lever, the rule being not to cause any undue panic or stress to the convicted. The straps were used to secure the arms and legs. This would stop the prisoner from thrashing around as he dropped and hung.

Most executions were quick and fast. Their aim was to carry out the job within 8 seconds or so.

The black cap placed on the judge's head gave the authority for Cyril to string many a man and woman onto the gallows. He was to be paid 10 guineas for his expertise and his rail fare would be covered too. All he needed to do, as part of his training was to put the straps on and get off that trap door fast. He needed a cool head as he didn't fancy falling in there too as the lever came down.

Cyril didn't have many close friends and he was careful who he told, as those who tried to befriend him he believed usually had their own macabre motives for getting into his head, and that would never do.

Oh, the tales he could have told around a bar, had he not been sworn into the official secrets act in the 1940's.

He was just an ordinary bloke and his drive was to bring an end to the convict's life; with as little distress to the prisoner as possible. He felt he was the chosen one and took his role very seriously.

When alone he would channel conversations with the deceased. Most of them forgave and praised him for the ease in which he orchestrated their demise.

Cyril struggled with the females that he had dropped, as it felt wrong to him. He tried not to mentally channel conversations with them. He tried to block them out.

He would often, while bordering on sleep, have visions of the hangings and see them on the other side. Going about their business free of their sins.

If anyone would have assessed his mental health, I'm not sure what they would have said. He was never mentored or counselled.

There are those who may say he had an inflated sense of his own importance, and a deep need for admiration.

Cyril on the other hand would have argued that he had a deep sense of empathy, that's why he took control of the souls' passing's in such a swift and pain free way as possible.

One of the most disturbing cases he had had to orchestrate, was the hanging of Richard Moore. A master manipulator and money lender.

Richard had a cruel and narcissistic personality, a clever thinker and usually always one step ahead. A true beast was Richard Moore. He never quite knew what to make of this man.

A devil worshipper, a man that practiced the art of Black Magick. Enticing innocent young girls with the promise of a good wage and better education, a job for life.

All those girls had gone to the big house, but instead of the dream to better themselves, they all faced their demise with a blow straight through their heart from a dagger. A human sacrifice.

This man was relentless and had no remorse at all.

He had been found guilty of rape and murder. He had carried out bizarre acts of cruelty and devious practices all in the name of the Golden order.

Richard believed he was a great lord and the master of his lodge. There he ruled with iron fists and cunning.

He had calmly planned his next victims' demise as a dark wave of pleasure would overcome him. He took his satisfaction, as his cruel mind and sadistic thoughts thrilled him. A very unpredictable man. He even had the ability to make his executioner feel uncomfortable.

The court case had found that he was guilty on four counts of murder. All young women. There had also been girls that had gone missing, who were never found.

He was under suspicion for those crimes too but it had never been proven.

A worshipper of the Devil for all these years. The leader of an occultist pact, a following that had gone back in history, through his heritage.

Even as Cyril walked him that morning to

the gallows, Richard Moore never flinched. Not even when the straps were pulled around his wrist and ankles. Even mentioned that he had no need for the linen hood to be pulled over his head.

It was the memory of that smile. More of a twisted grin that haunted Cyril for the rest of his life. Cyril tried to avoid looking into this man's Icy cold eyes.

Richard goaded Cyril on. He was always going to have the last laugh. His last words to Cyril were that he would meet him in hell.

Cyril placed the rope with the leather strap, over his head, making sure the eye on the leather strap was placed just under his left jaw, an eery laugh chilled him to the bones, and as Cyril jumped swiftly away from the trap doors, there was a load bang and clanking as Richard fell.

His laugh relentless, until his neck snapped

and there was an unnerving quiet in the chamber as the life drained from his body. 2nd February 1946 Richard dropped to his death aged sixty-one.

He would often reflect on the poor souls he had helped to pass over to the afterlife. Swift and quick. He believed that he would meet with these beings on the other side. So, a job to do and a job done well, to his very own satisfaction.

He prayed he would never have to meet the spirit of Richard Moore ever again. Still unnerved by the last words he had spoken to him.

Cyril was a bit of a hermit. He loved his own company and would venture out on many a walk within the countryside near to where he lived.

It was on that sorry day, Cyril found himself in a great predicament. He had gone off for a walk that morning, the weather seemed fine when he set off.

Later on, as dusk set in a fog, like a blanket consumed the area he was hiking in. His vision impaired massively.

The best option he thought was to find a safe place and stay put. He was sure that the search parties would be alerted and he would be found within the next few hours or early in the morning at least.

As he was finding a place to shelter, he stumbled and fell a good few feet from where he was walking the ground had become precarious under foot, his footing slipped and as he dropped the agonising pain pierced his side as realised he had become staked on a broken tree branch.

The pain was excruciating and he struggled to keep still, he found his breaths coming quickly with panic and agony, he tried to find comfort without much hope impaled onto this shard of wood.

He was quickly losing consciousness and he was aware that if he wasn't found within the next hour or so, his chances of survival were not going to be good.

He started to drift in and out of consciousness, dreams of his career, that he had been so proud of, started to haunt his thoughts.

Visions in his mind as he walked many a soul to his execution invaded his thoughts.

Most were resigned and trusted him to make their passing an easy one. Many wondering what judgment they would face, when meeting their master.

One of the last thoughts were how his god complex had been in tatters when his services where no longer needed. Dismissed and relieved of his duties he was sent back to his dreary work in the colliery.

There was no mention of his conscientiousness. Not a word of how he had rid society of the dregs of this earth. Just a letter in the post from her majesty's government.

Nothing to reward him even though he had served his country in order that the convicts and low lives had been disposed of in such a swift and professional manner. Cyril had been so proud of his work and had no regrets, well not when he reasoned with himself anyway. There had been one he had dropped, who struggled, wriggled, and screamed his innocence.

Cyril had been quite shaken and disturbed, when his usual swift execution had gone wrong. The linen hood became trapped in the rope. The man fought and struggled on the rope for a minute or so. This had given Cyril quite a fright.

The case was one of a brutal assault on a

young girl, so he secretly thought the man had got his just deserts.

The convict was later to be found innocent as the assaults carried on, until the true culprit was caught later on. It's safe to say and sods law, that this real monsters end, was a swift one.

~~~

The alarm was raised by Cyril's wife when he didn't arrive home that night. A search party waited until the fog had cleared the following morning. Cyril was an experienced walker so they knew he would have taken refuge in a safe spot.

He would have taken refreshments with him. He would be cold but relieved to see the locals as they made their way to find him.

Cyril was found, by young Jo the baker's lad. A right old shock for the poor boy. The young man said that he was sure he had heard and seen two dark figures, hurrying away from the incident.

The coroner's verdict recorded the death as accidental.

Cyril, was a respected chap within the town. Well looked up to in the town for ridding the place of scum and the dregs of society.

A rumour circulated round the pub, that someone had tried to give Cyril a taste of his own medicine. Some con who had served his time and had a grudge to bear for the wrongful hanging of his mate. The rumours circulated but this was just speculation and was never proven.

The doubt was there though, no smoke without fire. Many thought it may have been a revenge killing after a man had swung in innocence.

Cyril never did get any recognition for his service to his country and went to his death a disappointed man.

# LADY ELEANOR

Eleanor had been brought up by aristocrats. Her parents, Edward and Theodora were aloof characters. She was raised mainly by nurse maids and a governess.

Her mother was a recluse, and rarely left her boudoir. Pacifying and soothing herself with laudanum to medicate her shattered nerves.

Her father, was a brute, a bully and an abuser who would use those around him as punch bags. Her brother Victor had been taught from an early age, the art of cruelty, and how to be lord of the manor. He had a very good teacher, his father. Eleanor had learned from being a small child, to retreat and stay away from her guardian. The man who had only his own pleasure and interests at heart.

There was no one to turn too from this abuse. A mother sick and drunk, a father, violent, a teacher of deviance. Repulsive and obsessive. Eleanor had tried on many occasions to parent her mother, as the roles were reversed but all in vain.

Trying with all her might to stop her, Theodora self-medicating, as it made her so withdrawn and sleepy. On the odd occasion or first thing in the morning she was a happy, talkative and an interesting woman but very soon the medicine would take hold and gradually the drug would calm her.

The doctor gave her medication to help but over the months and years she had become an addict; she had to recognise and want to help herself, she couldn't or wouldn't, she just shut herself away from everyone, even her children.

Their mother had an intense dislike to her brother, her very own son, she swore he was evil, and that he was of the Devils spawn, she was adamant that Satan had raped her. The doctors put this delusion down to her condition.

There was no doubt that Victor her brother had a cruel nasty disposition, encouraged by his father, but Eleanor knew how to keep him calm at times and how to redirect his short attention span and distract him.

The conclusion Eleanor drew as she got older, was it was down her mother's mental condition.

From a young age Eleanor had witnessed the extravagant parties. Her parents would throw excessive gatherings, for those who would do anything, to be part of this club. Well known within the circles of the rich and famous.

Guests, with perverse fantasies. A game not for the faint hearted. Dabbling in the arts of Black Magick. Performing seances and conjuring up dark forces. Eleanor's father was the master within this society.

Eleanor had been on the altar on more than one occasion, acting out the macabre, cruel game. Although always one to be spared. Victor, her brother started as a spectator and as his apprenticeship commenced, he was trained and taught, by one of the best.

The only outlet for Eleanor was her writing. She poured her heart out within her journals. Diaries that spoke to any brave heart, who dared to venture into those pages. It portrayed her inner most thoughts. Not recommended, to the delicate, as these stories could disturb and crush many an innocent mind. Her brother's friend Richard often stayed for the duration of the summer holidays. This is where her story became complicated. To make matters worse, she fell in love with him, between him and her brother she was now used as a pawn in a game. Abused by them both, a game of cunning and deception.

Play acting many parts. I can only try to paint a picture.

At these regular balls. People of a particular status would gather. They were strange types, they all had one thing in common. Money. Pursuers of adventure and with a wallet large enough to pay for it.

A society that could buy anything but for some reason, were never fulfilled. Always wanting more. An elite group, the chosen ones could only be initiated by those in high places.

This is where Eleanor, a person of goodness and virtue was put on a path that led to her into disfigurement.

Eleanor had collaborated with Antonia an actress, who was a regular visitor and participant of these games, through no fault of her own.

An actress who desired her freedom from these brutes. Between them they had collaborated to set fire to Wheatfield house. The place these sordid games took place. In an effort to try to put a stop to the many years of cruelty that her brother and his friend enjoyed inflicting. The games were getting out of control. A sacrifice of a poor innocent maid.

The night that changed everything for Eleanor, was when poor Edmund, an artist and dealer she had engaged. He was brought there the under the pretence that he was to restore some pieces of art work.

Goaded on by those two. He was to be bribed and initiated into the group. That night, when enough was enough. Both Eleanor and

Antonia set out to destroy that house of evil.

This was one of her guilty secrets, she purposely planned to kill and burn her brother and Richard in the fire.

Her diaries spoke volumes and all her life's secrets were carefully logged and recorded.

Eleanor was an elderly lady now. A spinster as she never could settle down with anyone after the abuse she had suffered as a young girl.

So, she had chosen to become a recluse and as the debts on her estate had increased, she had auctioned and sold off most of her possessions and had taken a much more modest abode, on the outskirts of Cheshire. Where she lived with her lady's maid. No longer embroiled within this group as she was no longer any use to them, she didn't have the same wealth, or status, her face was scarred, she hid from the public by wearing a black veil if she ever ventured out or received guests, which was extremely rare.

Eleanor had catalogued her diaries and put them in order. The entries which had been extremely painful for her as a young girl she reread with contempt.

The metaphorical walls that she had built around her in order to keep her sanity. Stories hidden for the last forty years or so were now going to be shared.

Decades of hiding from the tabloids just in case she would be exposed for her role in grooming young girls for her lover and brother for their macabre, twisted sexual games.

Her adeptness at engaging young women to trust her, manipulating and drawing people into the big house in the guise of fun and parties in order to recruit.

Drawing out people's secrets and hidden desires so as to shame them and lock them in. Mentally calculating. A way of surviving her own darkness and the chaos she had found herself entwined in.

Her planned escape, as she deftly set fire to each room. A deliberate and methodical plan. Antonia had pushed the oil lamp that had set the drapes alight but it had been Eleanor who ran from room to room taking great pleasure in setting the grand house alight.

The burns to her arms, neck and right side of her face were a small price to pay than to stay within that torture chamber. Even her singed auburn hair that would never grow back, was a small price to pay and was worth it.

Back to the present day, Eleanor had not been surprised when her physician had given her the news.

He had taken a blood sample from her and it was imminent she had developed skin cancer from the burns she had inflicted on herself.

He had a duty of care and he needed to explain that the development of malignant tumours from chronic burns, which were extremely rare. It usually took around 20 to 30 years which had been much longer in Eleanor's case so she felt blessed in some strange way.

It had taken form in a degeneration of her burn scars. Eleanor with trepidation asked what would happen next. With a sense of gloom consuming her as her premonition was correct. A strange feeling of relief consumed her, as her life's struggle would now be coming to an end.

The doctor explained she would be sent to the very best Chemotherapist in Britain. This doctor worked endlessly and believed that cancer would eventually succumb to these new drugs.

Anti-cancer drugs had made their entrance in the 1940's and The Christie hospital was known around the world for its pioneering work.

The skin on her face and neck had become angry again, just like at the time she had burnt. Red, blotchy and ulcerated.

Eleanor knew there was nothing they could do for her, even before the consultant talked through her options. Eleanor decided there and then that enough was enough and she would surrender her time on this planet.

Her thoughts of her past and the life she had led made her reflect. Bitter from the abuse she had suffered at the hands of Victor her brother and Richard her lover.

The parents who had never protected her. A father too busy with his debaucherous ways, a tutor for his son. A mother weak and mild, not able to stand up to this brute. Sorrow for her mother, god knows what she went through.

Reflecting on her own misdeeds. Regretting those sordid games that she had become wrapped up in. Befriending young teens, knowing that they were about to have their innocence stolen from them by that hideous bunch.

As Eleanor placed her journals in a box in the hall, she reached for the telephone and dialled 999.

She would confess to everything, as at the end of the day, her time was up and she would rather take her punishment. What a twist of fate.

Richard had swung, too late, it should have happened years ago. she had been glad in a perverse way. He couldn't abuse or torture another now he had been hung and dropped.

Eleanor rang the local newspapers too; her precious box of diaries would now be exposed to the outside world.

Notoriety she hadn't wanted, but justice she did, after living a hermit's existence for years and years. It was the right time she thought.

A heart that had been turned cold, even the burns could never warm her.

A peace and a gladness all this was finally over.

Now in her seventies and in very poor health, she now painstakingly and methodically placed the leather-bound volumes wrapped in brown paper parcels tied up with string. Carefully putting her affairs in order.

A life story that once had been locked away. Upon her death would all be exposed.

Her confession to all the wrongs she had done and what others had done to her.

Once exposed many would fall and many would get their just deserts. No one could touch her now. This was her time.

# ALICE HALL

Alice was blessed with an attractive face, an hour glass shape, who knew how to turn on the charm. A cheeky and flighty young thing. As a little girl, had fancied herself as a ballet dancer.

Twirling and pirouetting in front of her friends. A special treat for her was to spend an evening at the cinema. There, she would watch Hollywood actresses and take lessons from their performances.

It wasn't that difficult to join a dancing and drama school and with her charm and good looks, she started to give performances at her local theatre.

Alice was a natural on the stage and eventually found herself playing the lead roles. Many a man would wait for her at the stage door with flowers and gifts in the hope to win her heart.

Her family had come from a poor background but they all had the arts in common, her mother played beautifully on the piano, and was also a very good artist.

Alongside her acting talents she had a way of teasing and flirting with the opposite sex and she would have men eating out of the palm of her hand.

Sod's law as usual because the one she really wanted the most was the married man.

Alice was wooed and charmed by her lover, He said all the right things, showering her with gifts and expensive clothes. He took her to the best dress shops of the time and she looked a million dollars.

Her life had seemed so much better since meeting him, she adored him. Freely giving herself, in exchange for the lavish lifestyle, fancy restaurants and week days away.

The only time she didn't get chance to see him was at the weekends, she would sigh and push those thoughts out of her head because she was pretty sure he was playing happy families, with his wife and children.

She couldn't think too much about that or it would make her feel bitter and jealous, so she changed her mindset.

Especially, as he promised her that when the time was right, he would leave his unhappy marriage and they would spend their life together.

Her goal would be complete, she would become Mrs M.

The sex was amazing, especially as it was

forbidden. The way he would sneak out to steal an intimate hour or two. How desire can make someone grateful for those tiny stolen moments.

Alice believed his stories, every damn one of them. Every lie. He was very good at convincing her, he gave her no reason to doubt him. Well, M was a good talker, a natural.

A very successful business man, she only ever referred to him by the initial of his surname. M. Her way of protecting him.

M, never did anything wrong, not in his eyes anyway. It was none of his wife's business what he did when she wasn't there. His wife he adored, she reminded him of a goddess, he put her on a pedestal the, virgin queen, not to be tarnished. The mother of his children.

Alice was loving, voluptuous and different, she adored him, she showed him all the time. Alice never made any demands on his family time, he was sure his mistress, enjoyed the stolen moments just as much as he did.

M was much older than Alice, he could show her what she had not experienced yet. A lover that took her to the most sensual of places. The guilty pleasures of lust.

Some days she wished she had never met him and that she had walked away when he told her he was married but she didn't. and that was that. Now it was too late as, she loved him and he loved her. He had told her so.

Alice had seen his wife once at the office. They say you can find the truth out about a man by meeting his wife. His dependencies and his weaknesses. The wife was elegant, composed and very beautiful, but aloof Alice thought.

Alice, reflected about love, and what it was. She couldn't quite work it out, all she could see was that it caused her heartache and pain for the most of the time, with a smattering of happiness.

During those stolen moments with Alice, M couldn't leave her alone, was it the way she looked at him, he thought, those smouldering brown eyes or was it the way her lips filled the air, as her gentle sighs increased his desire for her. That forbidden embrace.

M loved his wife, she was precious, he would never tell her. Why would he, he would never hurt her or his girls. After all. Everyone was happy, no need to upset the boat.

Alice could ignite something that his wife could never do. Those raging fires of lust. Alice was looked after, after all, she had the best of him, he thought.

The affair carried on for quite a long time, until Alice decided that age was becoming an issue for her, she didn't want to be a spinster so she set about how she would trick M into making her a mum, she was going to have a baby before it was too late. Life's clock was ticking by after all.

Alice chose her evening with care and as she set out to seduce the man of her life, the future father of her child, her future husband, the thought of what she was about to do made her feel wild and passionate with desire.

He would now have no choice but to leave his wife, he adored his two children. Both girls, he often talked about them. Alice didn't mind what sex the baby would be as M would adore it anyway, as he did his other two and if it was a boy, then that would be even better she thought.

It was only a matter of time before M would leave his wife for Alice. Well, he was always showing Alice around luxury properties, promising her that would be where they would live once they were together properly.

Alice pushed thoughts of the wife and

family away, it didn't concern her. They didn't matter when Alice was with M.

He had a small apartment in the city, the one that he used when he was working late at the office. The very one he used when he was tied up with overtime. Not to disturb his wife.

Alice would stay with him usually after the show or when they had been on a night out, never at weekends. No, weekends, they were a no go. So, she filled her time shopping.

M would tell her to buy something nice as he would like to see her wearing it. He was so kind, so why did she feel so lonely at times.

It was those horrible nights, when he wouldn't call her and the arrangements would be cancelled last minute, and how she smiled and said it was fine and it didn't matter, when it did matter. It mattered to her. Why was her time less precious than his? The small apartment would never do for a baby and Alice wouldn't want to bring a child up in the City. Anyway, she planned that she would persuade M to look at properties within the suburbs, places where there would be some nice schools and parks for the child to play in.

Alice was definitely with child, she had missed a couple of periods and although she hadn't felt sick, her breasts felt different, fuller. M had even mentioned that they felt different to touch, more sensual he had murmured into her ear as he lay with her. This had to be the right time to tell him, as they had made love and were lay romantically within each other's arms.

So, she did.

He said all the right things. He was so very happy and held her even closer. Very convincing. This was the best day in her whole life.

Finally, she had sealed the deal. How clever of her she thought. She loved him so much, and now their life would be perfect together.

She could give up work as a bookkeeper, the job helped her to pay her keep as she had a small room in a local guest house, and she would become the new Mrs M.

Her landlady was an absolute battle axe and she would now be able to tell her to stuff her grimy, stuffy room, where the sun doesn't shine, as she no longer required residency in that grotty overpriced hovel.

So proud, that she could parade her handsome lover to the whole world and she would become the perfect wife of Mr M. What bliss.

She snuggled closer into him and doing what she did best, made love to him once again.

They slept exhausted and content.

What happened next was totally unexpected. The seed he had planted in her belly was not the only seed he planted that day.

This was the note she found on the bed when she woke:

*My darling Alice,*

*I hope you won't be too disappointed but I can't go through with this. I have more than loved our liaisons and you are a truly gorgeous and sensual woman.*

*However, it wouldn't be right to leave my girls. I'm sure you understand. There is some money in this envelope, I know a good doctor who is very discreet and reliable with these sorts of things.*

*Here is his business card.*

*I'm sure you will agree that it's best if we don't see each other for a while at least until after this unfortunate incident is dealt with.*

*M. x*


Rage! Her dreams now shattered, fragments of her fantasy, smashed into irrepairable shards all over the place. How could she put these pieces back together again into some kind of order, she couldn't think straight. How had she misjudged their relationship? How could he? This was cruel. He had told her he loved her, she had waited for him and given him the best part her life.

He couldn't possibly leave her not now especially. How could she keep the baby, the landlady would throw her out onto the streets for bringing shame to her lodging house.

Desperately she tried calling his work place for days on end. His young secretary would inform her, that he was either out on business and she would pass the message on, but he never got back in touch.

They say there is a thin line between love and hate and she was torn between the two.

Alice thought she would march straight round to his house and tell his wife what he had been up to, she could tell her the very dates and times that M had been working late or sealing a deal or two in the afternoons when he should have been in the office.

Thinking about it, and on second thought she realised it would not help the situation, so once again, she put herself and her feelings in second place as knowing deep down, she had just been his bit of fun.

So, on an icy, nippy, January morning, frosty and freezing, Alice caught the early morning bus into Piccadilly Manchester.

It was an old Victorian office block very close to Deansgate, a private entrance, she climbed a dingy musty stairway.

A middle-aged man in a white coat, guided her into a room with a wooden table covered in a white sheet.

There were various, steel tools laid neatly on a tray, alongside a rubber tube of some sort and some gloves. There were some methylated spirits, cotton wool and some gauze. A nauseating smell of bleach reached her nostrils.

The doctor asked her did she have the money and she nervously handed him the fat envelope containing more than she earned in five weeks.

Wishing M was there, shaking and feeling petrified, the man coldly instructed to go and empty her bladder and then take off her undergarments and lie on the table.

He told her to put her heels together and drop her knees apart. He looked at her from under his round spectacles and ordered her to keep still. Alice explained that she had not had a period for three months. Desperately trying to make conversation, in the hope of easing her situation.

She was instructed not to make a sound,

so not to draw attention to his office or to this procedure he was about to carry out.

He helped her on to her back and placed a pillow under her head. As the doctor raised her knees and examined her, she felt the urgent need to cover herself. Exposed.

He seemed to be taking a rather long time, down there, touching and peering through a magnifying glass.

Unnerved and without a chaperone, he carefully inserted an icy, metal speculum inside her. It was cold and uncomfortable as she heard the mechanism of the tool, extend into her inners.

Nothing though, to the pain of that thin icy rod, gently and expertly being guided, threaded through thick gauze, into her cervix. A miscarriage was now to be induced.

A terrifying experience, she lay uncovered. As this man worked conscientiously between her legs.

When he had finished. He told her to get dressed and informed her that there would be some cramping and bleeding and she was given antibiotics just in case there was a fever.

A day or so later Alice woke during the night with horrendous pelvic cramps, she felt nauseous and faint and she had been sweating profusely.

Blood was dripping down from her in clots, she stuffed tissue and sanitary towels between her legs in an effort to stem the blood, her bed sheets and mattress saturated with her haemorrhage.

Alice had placed a mop bucket near her bed in the eventuality that this might happen and sitting precariously on the side of her bed, she emptied the contents of her uterus, splattering, scarlet, brown and bloody into the cold metal tin.

Alice aborted her baby. She never did go on to have any children afterwards, as her private abortionist had put paid to that.

On knocking on Alice's door persistently for her overdue rent, Mrs Gulliver her landlady was shocked and traumatised when she found Alice's lifeless body and foetus tipped over on to the bedsit floor.

# THE JOURNEY

All four found themselves in a train carriage. It was misty and smoky as the locomotive strained, puffed and chugged away to its destination.

They took their seats, in silence, not sure what to expect. Very different characters each and every one of them.

Not one of them would have particularly chosen to spend time with the other, as they were all from very different mortal walks of life.

As the train pulled away from the station and the journey commenced; the man with the very fine suit who carried a violin case, regarded the slim woman with red hair and a queenly air, and wondered why she had chosen to wear that old fashioned, expensive pillar box hat, with a black veil obscuring and covering her face.

An attractive young woman wearing a red shift dress. gazed on the middle-aged man with the grey gabardine overcoat and flat cap, with interest. He, totally engrossed, reading his detective novel. Never raising his eyes from those pages, he took no notice of her in the slightest.

The trip commenced and just as human nature prevails and as uncomfortable as it was, they carried on their journey in silence.

Just to break the silence, a ticket inspector entered the carriage and informed them to collect their belongings as they would be arriving at their destination within a few minutes.

The train screeched to a halt, the intensity of the steam surrounded them, obscuring their peripheral vision.

Directly in front of them, what looked like a station door beckoned them in with the comfort of a bright light. The ticket master, ushered them in and through a hallway, into a waiting room.

The room itself was pretty plain, not somewhere one would want to wait too long. there were wooden seats offering nothing in the way of comfort.

A large ornate clock ticked and sounded its chimes as all four waited patiently for the grand door to open for them.

As they sat waiting to enter the door to their final destination each one took time to reflect upon their life.

The Temperance Tale

# JUSTICE AND JUDGMENT

L et's start with Samuel, as he was the first character in the book. As we already established he had a cheerful and charming persona, a charmer in his own right. Gaining the confidence and trust of others, quite easily.

Charming his boss, his intention had always been to aim high for what he wanted in life, he believed that nothing was out of his reach. Devising a plan, trusting that his mind would figure a way to achieve his goals.

He knew that if he won Edwin over, he could concentrate on winning the hand of his daughter. Eva hadn't been blessed with looks as such and Edwin knew, he needed a husband for his girl. There were not many suitors queuing up at his door. So, when Samuel his loyal manager and good friend asked for her hand in marriage, it was a no brainer really.

Samuel was over the moon. Once his father-in-law passed away, he had more money than he could ever hope for. It gave him a freedom to allow him to do what he wanted and he had a kind heart and helped many out. Helping to pay back his good fortune.

With this came his biggest regret as he blamed himself for his daughter's death. Had he not been rich, that Freddie boy would never have given his daughter, Grace the time of day, he was quite sure of that.

~~~

Cyril took his time in the waiting room, to look back on his life. He had married quite young and had no children. He was thankful for that.

There were only three people who knew of his important job and that was his employer down the colliery, his wife and his old friend from school. Others speculated and rumours circled.

He believed he had served his King and then later on his Queen well. He did believe that he should have been knighted or at least had more recognition for his duty to the British Isles.

The death penalty had ceased under his service and Cyril believed this to be a grave mistake on the governments part. Yes he did believe a couple of his convicts had been innocent and he was haunted by that thought.

However, on the whole and in a matter of speaking, the death penalty did serve as a massive deterrent for most people. He predicted that life in Britain would not be better off without it.

Well, he couldn't change his path, so he could only have those conversations with himself on the matters that weighed on his conscience.

~~~

Eleanor was about to expose each and every one of the group. A case would explode and it would hit all the major tabloids in the world news. Her brother and his friend's sorcery, debauchery and disgrace were about to be exposed in many newspapers.

People in very high positions would be on all the front covers of all the tabloids and magazines too. Many would be prosecuted to the embarrassment of families in high places.

How Richard her abuser went to the gallows for the murdering that young servant girl, who

Eleanor found out cruelly by her brother that she was her very own child. Conceived during her brothers abuse as they acted out a sacrifice during one of their evil games.

Eleanor had no remorse for causing the fire that killed her brother. She had paid the price and worn the facial scars as a permanent reminder for the rest of her life.

There was no reason to disclose the girl's parentage as she had been raised by an older couple who loved her dearly. It would never do the girls memory or parents any good to know of her conception and her evil genes.

So, she mindfully omitted this information from her journals. The girl's family would never know. She had protected her daughter.

She regretted the grooming of the young girls and of Edmund the art restorer, she had lured to the big house under the pretence of restoring some paintings.

Later, to find out that he had taken his own life to protect his niece from Richard. A terrible state of affairs she thought. She still blamed Victor and Richard for this as she would have never stooped this low had it not been for those bullies.

Eleanor's justification for her actions and her conscience was clear as far as she was concerned. After all, she had suffered for years shutting herself off from the world to hide her mental and physical scars.

~~~

Alice had betrayed another woman, by seducing her husband. M was quite a few years older than her and although she thought that she had been clever trapping such a fine catch.

A pregnancy planned on her part so that he would leave his wife and children.

M was always one step ahead; his intention

was that he was never going to marry her.

All he had wanted, she reflected was the fun and excitement of the affair, no strings, no ties, at the end of the day he thought she seemed happy enough. She never had the confidence to voice her truth.

Was her self-esteem that low, to be treated like a door mat, just in case he might have finished the relationship. Well, he did anyway.

So, all was meant to be, she concluded.

He didn't have the need for more children. Alice had been devastated by this news and she knew that she wasn't strong enough and didn't have the support to bring a baby up on her own.

Her landlady at her digs where she was staying would never allow her to bring a child up there.

It had all been her own doing and so very complicated. Grateful for M organising her back street abortion.

Devastated when the abortion was carried out. The shame to be in the hands of that butcher in Manchester, the sadness and the guilt as her baby fell from her body.

Her conscience was not clear but if she could take any comfort at all it was that she would at some point take her role once more as mother to her unborn child.

# THE LAST DAY

The four jolted back from the reverie of their reflections to the sound of the ticking clock above the grand ornate double doors.

All four had decided that they had been dealt the card of injustice and judgment. They also realised that each and every one of them had also dealt that card to another.

An internal, inner awakening, the final karma of weighing and measuring the rights and wrongs they felt had been inflicted on themselves and others. Their own Judge.

The deafening sound of silence fell upon

the room, as the ornate clock stopped ticking as the elaborate grand door that had once been closed to them, slowly opened to welcome them in.

'For It is only a free man, who pleases himself'.

Printed in Great Britain
by Amazon

61697007R00057